TREETOP TWINS

WILDERNESS ADVENTURES

The Twins Follow
a Polar Bear

Cressida Cowell

Hodder
Children's
Books

There are four snowy owls in this
book. Can you find them all?

The snow gleamed and dazzled
as the sun glinted off the ice.
The Treetop family have
transformed their time machine
into a snowmobile, and they have
travelled, not back in time, but
far, far away, to the Arctic.

It was so cold the wind nipped your nose like a bee sting. The Treetop family were looking for the largest land carnivore in the world – the magnificent polar bear.

Tulip spotted a snowy owl. Asha spotted an Arctic fox. Alfie spotted an orca. But nobody had spotted any polar bears.

'Look!' said Professor Penelope excitedly. 'There are bear prints in front of us!'

Professor Penelope bent down to measure the bear prints.

'Let's follow them!' said Ted.
He wandered on ahead, looking
through his binoculars.

'Careful, Ted!' warned Professor Pablo. 'Polar bears are wonderful animals, but they can be very dangerous!'

Ted stomped back, cross. 'I can see there are no polar bears nearby!'

'Polar bears have black skin, and their fur is not white – it is actually transparent,' said Asha. 'In this snowy landscape, it looks white because it reflects the sunlight. You might find it hard to spot a polar bear...'

But suddenly, Ted DID spot
something. Out on the ice was a
mother polar bear and her two
little cubs! The mother was very

still, watching a hole in the ice,
hoping to catch a seal. Her cubs
were playing nearby, sliding on
their tummies in the snow.

'How exciting!' said Professor Penelope. 'A mother and her cubs!'

One of the cubs ran off across the ice. The mother called out to it. But the cub did not listen.

It ran and ran...
...and then suddenly there was a loud...
CRACK!
Followed by an even louder...
SPLASH!

YOOOOWWW!

The cub yelled as the ice gave
way and it was plunged into the
freezing cold water beneath.

'Oh no!' said Professor Penelope,
looking through her binoculars.

'That cub is very young – it may not know how to swim yet!'

Whatever should they do?

The mother bear was frantic with worry. She ran over to the edge of the ice and called out to her baby. Her other cub was so scared, it climbed up on to its mother's back.

'Should we help the cub?' asked Asha.

'I don't think we can,' said Professor Pablo. 'The mother is so frightened, she might attack us.'

'Wait!' said Professor Penelope. 'Look...I think Mum might be giving her cub its first swimming lesson.'

And it was true...While the baby polar bear splashed around, trying to reach the safety of the ice, the mother looked on, and called out to her cub. And sure enough, the splashing soon began to look like swimming, and the swimming brought the cub to the edge of the ice.

The baby polar bear pulled itself out of the water, shook itself off and ran to join its mother. They nuzzled each other lovingly, then the cub and its mother and sibling all wandered off together across the ice.

'Phew,' panted Professor Penelope, as the Treetop family watched the polar bears disappear. 'I'm glad none of you took a plunge into that icy water! Just watching that cub has made me feel cold. Let's go home...'

And they all went back to their cosy icehouse for dinner.

Night-time in the Arctic. Back at the icehouse, the professors made notes about polar bear populations and habitats, while the Treetop twins played at sledging down the ice hills until it was time to go to bed.

Because human children are not so very different from bear cubs.

'And polar bear parents are just like OUR parents,' said Ted as he

got into bed. 'Sometimes they
fuss at us, but it is only because
they want us to be safe.'

'Yes, and they want you to
go to sleep too!' said Professor
Penelope, as she turned out the
light. 'I bet those tired baby polar
bears are fast asleep already...'

ASHA'S FACTS ABOUT POLAR BEARS

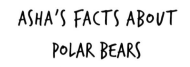

Polar bears have black skin and although their fur appears white, it is actually transparent.

The word Arctic comes from the Greek word 'arktos', meaning bear.

Polar bears are the largest land carnivores on the planet.